To Fred —
Touch the sky!

Burt Bagent
2/94

All rights reserved
Published by Wordsong
Boyds Mills Press, Inc.
A Highlights Company
910 Church Street
Honesdale, Pennsylvania 18431

Publisher Cataloging-in-Publication Data
Bagert, Brod.
        Let me be the boss : poems for kids to perform / by Brod Bagert ; illustrated by G.L. Smith.
[48] p. : ill. ; cm.
Summary: A collection of humorous poems to read aloud and perform.
ISBN 1-56397-099-6
1. Children's poetry, American. [1. American Poetry.] I. Smith, G.L., ill.
II. Title.
811.54—dc20   1992
Library of Congress Catalog Card Number: 91-91408

First edition, 1992
Book designed by Tim Gillner
The text of this book is set in 16-point Clearface Regular.
The illustrations are pen and ink.
Distributed by St. Martin's Press
Printed in the United States of America

10 9 8 7 6 5 4 3 2

Let Me Be...
The Boss

Poems for Kids to Perform

by Brod Bagert

Illustrated by G. L. Smith

WORDSONG

To "Ma B"
The best mom a kid ever had.
B. B.

Contents

Gorilla

Big gorilla
Hairy gorilla
Gorilla looking sad,
The short one with the belly
Reminds me of my dad.

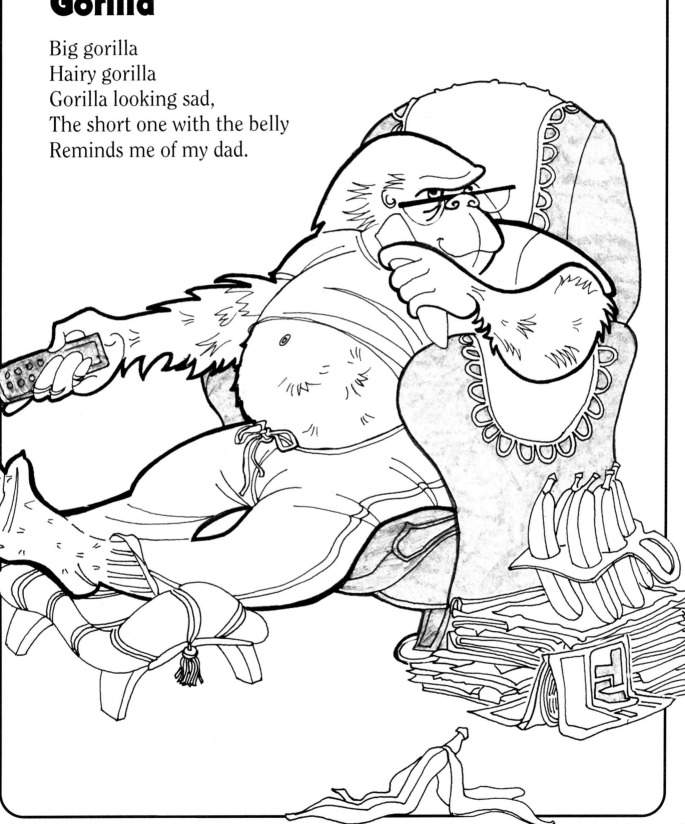

The Boss

I'm just a little kid
Not even four foot two
I weigh less than sixty pounds
And I'm half the size of you.

I do everything you say
I don't talk back or fight
So I wish you'd stop and ask yourself—
Are you sure you're always right?

Like at the supper table,
I feel like such a sinner
Just because I want dessert
Before I finish dinner.

Bedtime's eight o'clock,
What's wrong with eight-fifteen?
Is there some evil magic
That would turn my eyebrows green?

If you would just cooperate
Our words would never cross,
Life would be so wonderful
If you'd let me be the boss.

Birdseed

It didn't work.
I planted birdseed in the ground
And wild weeds sprouted all around.
I know it sounds a bit absurd
But I couldn't grow a single bird.

Fair Warning

There's an alligator in that bathroom.
He has big teeth
And he likes to eat.
So, please . . . be very careful
When you lift the toilet seat.

Poor Ron's Allergy

No dogs
No cats
No hamsters
No guinea pigs
No squirrels . . .
If I had to have an allergy
Why wasn't it to girls.

My Handsome Prince

Out there . . . somewhere,
There's someone just for me.

A boy who'll reach maturity
Without a blanket for security.

A boy who'll be strong when things are a mess
And won't hide behind his mother's dress.

A boy who'll hug me close and tight
Even when we've had a fight.

I know someday my prince will come,
I just hope he doesn't suck his thumb.

The Even Trade

He's a wonderful little brother,
He hardly ever picks his nose,
And if you make him wear his shoes
He won't lick between his toes.

He'll probably never eat another caterpillar
And that's not a real tattoo,
Why . . . with a little soap and water
He'll smell as good as new.

Even if your mom says no
It's still a guarantee,
You can keep my little brother
And get your hamster back for free.

Dr. Womback's Needle

There'll be footsteps any second now
And through the door they'll burst,
Dr. Womback's needle
In the hands of Dr. Womback's nurse!

Now this will pinch a little, she'll say
As I see the shiny steel
Of a fifteen-foot-long needle
She claims I'll hardly feel.

Someday I'll be big and strong
And she couldn't hurt me if she tried,
But now . . . I'm just a little kid . . .
And I think I'm gonna cry.

The Night Visitor

The creature in the closet is ugly
He has yellow eyes that stare,
But if he stares his eyes at me
I'll tell him I don't care.

The creature in the closet is dangerous
He has claws and teeth that cut,
But if he shows his teeth to me
I'll smile and say so what.

I used to be afraid
Until I grew up strong,
So now I sleep alone at night
But . . . not for very long.

The Famous Purple Poka Bear

My big brother
Taught me about bears.

You can tell each different kind of bear
By the color of its hair.
There are black bears . . .
And brown bears . . .
And polar bears as white as snow . . .
And the famous purple poka bear
With pink dots on the top half
And purple dots below.

My big brother tells me everything,
Everything a kid should know.

Alexander's Breakfast

Alexander woke up **hungry**
So he ate three eggs
A slice of ham
Crisp whole-wheat toast and apple jam,
Fresh orange juice to wash it down
But on his face was still a frown.

Then a pile of pancakes
Hot with syrup
Sausage links and Danish cake,
Then his mother said,
Alexander,
Don't you ever take a break?
Then he ate some cherries,
He ate the pits,
Hot oatmeal, grits, and bacon bits,
Twelve green bananas,
A cold sliced pear,
And then he started on the chair.
I don't know how that boy was able
To eat six chairs and the kitchen table,
But he ate each leg down to the floor
And started chewing on the door.
He ate the pictures off the wall,
The old green carpet in the hall,
Window curtains,
Burglar bars,
A two-wheel bike
And the family cars.

Then he smiled and said,
Mom, thanks a bunch . . .
What time should I be home for lunch?

Tiger Cubs

The tiger's eyes are black as coal,
The tiger's walk is smooth and bold,
The tiger's heart is strong and brave,
But tiger cubs still misbehave.

Llama

A Real Poem

Llama llama llama llama
Llama llama llama.

Llama llama llama llama
Llama llama llama.

Llama.
Llama!
Llama . . .

MOOOOOOOOOOOO!

Llama?

Llama llama llama llama
Llama llama llama.

Fancy Restaurants

Sorry, young man,
We have no hamburgers,
But wouldn't you like to try
A hot, juicy slice of octopus pie?
Or, if you wish, a steaming dish
Of earthworm slime and jellyfish?
Pickled frog eyes?
Boiled eel?
Alligator gizzard and lizard tail?
Green fungus and spider legs
With a bowl of crushed green garden snail?

This yummy food is all for you
Don't let it go to waste,
It's fun to try new things to eat,
Won't you take a little taste?

My Uncle Jake

My uncle Jake is a little weird,
Mom says he'll never change,
That even when he was a kid
He acted kind of strange.

He told me the moon is a growl in his heart,
That the wind is a trusted friend,
That birds are born to play in the air
But rivers must rush to an end.

I wonder about my uncle Jake . . .
When he stayed at our house last night,
All the stuff he said was strange . . .
I guess my mom is right.

Always Be Polite
When You Boss an Allosaurus

There was this giant skeleton,
Thirty feet from tail to head—
And I bet they couldn't make him brush
Before he went to bed.

His teeth were long and pointy,
As sharp as they could be—
And I'd like to see them try to tell him
Not to watch TV.

Stop that, you naughty dinosaur,
I've had about enough of you.
Then **CRRRRUNCH!**
One less bossy grown-up
To tell us what to do.

The Dinosaur Difference

They walked on the land
And flew in the air
And swam in the water of an inland sea,
But now they're gone
Cuz dinosaurs
Were not as smart as you or me.

Mini Monsters

Some dinosaurs were small,
Two feet tall was big as they could get.
Look, Mom! A tiny dinosaur!
Pleeeeeeeeeeeeeease?
Can I keep it for a pet?

Poor Dinosaur Children

If I were a dinosaur,
With big long dinosaur feet,
It would only take two steps
For me to cross the street.

If I were a dinosaur
I'd grow and I'd grow and I'd grow
Till I could smush a motorcycle
With just my little toe.

If I were a dinosaur,
With a dinosaur stomach and a dinosaur eye,
I could catch and eat an elephant
And still have room for pie.

But I'm glad I'm not a dinosaur,
With a tiny dinosaur head,
Poor dinosaur children had no books, or moms
To read to them in bed.

Good Ideas

If the wheel squeaks
It's time to oil it.

When the egg is soft
You may want to boil it.

If the floor is clean
Try not to spoil it.

When you have to go,
Please!
Use the toilet.

First Things First

I'm gonna *throw* farther,

I'm gonna *go* faster,

I'm gonna *bump* harder,

I'm gonna *jump* higher,

I'm gonna get good
At lots and lots of new things,
If only I could find someone
To help me tie my shoestrings.

A True Story

Honest, Mom!
I was headed straight for home,
I didn't even stop to play
But this big old flying saucer
Landed in my way,
And before I had a chance to run
Out jumped two little guys,
And the green one zapped me with a ray
That shot out from his eyes.
It's all a little fuzzy . . . ahhhhhh . . .
I must have bumped my head,
But the next thing I remember
I was strapped down on this bed,
And we were zooming into outer space
Halfway to the moon,
And I had to think of something
And I had to do it soon,
So I grabbed the steering wheel
And I turned it back around
And I flew through lots of clouds and stuff
And crashed into the ground.
Then I hurried straight for home,
I didn't even stop to talk,
So you see, Mom . . .
There's a real good reason
That I got home after dark.

Happy New Year

Now is the moment,
So open up your eyes,
Turn your face
To the cold night skies,
Watch the midnight rocket,
For as its fire flies,
The new year comes
And the old year dies.

Skinny Minnie

She's not what she would seem,
This sparkle frizzy Minnie,
Someday she'll be a young man's dream
Though for now she's kind of skinny.

Brothers

One brother's name was Thackery
The other's name was Zackery.

While Thackery was rickety,
His fortitude quite crickety,
Old Zack, he was unsinkable
To give up was unthinkable.

Thackery was shivery
His hands were always quivery,
But Zackery worked skillfully
Completing each job willfully.

There is no cause for quibbling,
Said Zackery to his sibling,
We're not like the others
Who call themselves brothers,
Affection they claim by being the same,
But our claim is stiffer . . .
We share how we differ.

Zebra

White stripes on black
Or black stripes on white
I can never tell what's right,
Does darkness follow after day
Or does day come after night?

How to Say NO Politely
When a Lion Invites You to Lunch

Dear Mr. Lion,

I know you wouldn't eat me,
You'd have to be a dummy
To gobble up a little kid
Too small to fill your tummy.

Besides . . .
Grandma always says
I'm sweet as icing on the cake,
So if you made a meal of me
You might get a stomachache.

And even if your claws
Are sharp as surgical devices,
I know you'd be real careful
Not to cut me into slices.

So thank you for inviting me
To lunch with you today,
I'm sure it would be lots of fun
If you and I could play,
And I honestly don't doubt the truth
Of anything you say,
But . . . you look a little hungry
So . . . ***I'M GONNA STAY AWAY.***

Sincerely,
A Smart Kid

Open Up

Some things are pretty tricky.
Did you ever wonder why
The sun gets big and orange
At the bottom of the sky?

What grows hair on Daddy's face?
Who put black in tar?
Where do locusts come from?
How heavy is a star?

Well don't let questions scare you
Cuz you don't have far to look,
The whole world is your crystal ball
When you open up a book.

Under Stepping Stones

I found two worms and a beetle bug
And tiny ants with tiny white eggs,
And a funny-looking orange thing
With at least a hundred legs.

It was just a flat old rock
All chipped and cracked and worn,
You'd never know that underneath
So much was going on.

Eons Hours and Wind

Clouds come and go,
Children of the hours,
Towers of vapor . . .
Blown away in the wind.

Mountains come and go,
Children of the ages,
Towers of stone . . .
Blown away in the wind.

The Jumping Clown

When I think about my life
And remember that I'll die,
I jump with all my might
And try to touch the sky!

But of course . . . I never reach it,
So after I descend,
I wait until the laughter stops
And jump back up again.

Brod Bagert is a poet who lives in New Orleans. A popular speaker in schools, teachers' workshops, and conferences, he advocates performing as a way for children to learn to love poetry. Mr. Bagert is the father of four children.

Gerald Smith has a BFA in illustration from Pratt Institute. He has created illustrations for numerous magazines, books, and textbooks.
He lives in New York City.